The Legend of Old Abe

A Civil War Eagle

Written by Kathy-jo Wargin and Illustrated by Laurie Caple

About the Legend of Old Abe

There are many versions of the legend of Old Abe, the eagle who captured the spirit of a country at war as well as the imaginations of people who wanted to believe that he was indeed a soldier of war.

As you read the story, please pay special attention to the wonderful visuals. Artist Laurie Caple's great attention to detail and historical accuracy is reflected throughout. You may notice the soldiers of Old Abe's unit (the Eighth Wisconsin Volunteer Infantry) began their service in gray uniforms, yet later they are depicted wearing blue uniforms. During the Civil War, there was variety in the uniforms worn by the Union soldiers. Another item of interest is that Old Abe was carried by several different eagle-bearers, dedicated soldiers who cared for and protected the eagle.

Many years after his war service, Old Abe died from illness due to smoke inhalation from a fire at the capitol building. Today, a replica of Old Abe exists in the Assembly Chamber at the Wisconsin State Capitol Building.

Old Abe remains an important historical figure in Wisconsin, where the facts of his life (and the legend that grew around them) will remain in the hearts of those who have heard his tale, and believed in the courage, dedication, and loyalty of a bird from northern Wisconsin. May you come to know Old Abe through this legend, and may you explore the many other versions of this story as well as the historical facts of his full life.

—Kathy-jo Wargin

A young boy and his grandfather walked into the Assembly Chamber at the Wisconsin State Capitol Building. It was as quiet as a library and more beautiful than a grand ballroom, and at the front of the room was a replica of an American bald eagle named Old Abe. The boy took a closer look at the eagle as his grandfather began this tale.

Long ago in the big woods of Wisconsin, Daniel McCann and his wife greeted a visitor named Chief Sky. He was from the Lac du Flambeau band of Indians, and traveling to Chippewa Falls with a load of goods to trade.

In exchange for a bushel of corn, Chief Sky gave the McCann family a young bald eagle that had been captured near the Flambeau River. It was not much larger than a fat hen, and its feathers were the color of dull brown mud. Even so, the eaglet delighted the McCann children very much.

During the day the children went in search of rabbits and mice for the young eagle's food. In the evenings, when Mr. McCann played lively tunes on his fiddle, it hopped around and spread its wings as if dancing to the music. The McCanns adored their new pet, and they gave the bird a good home.

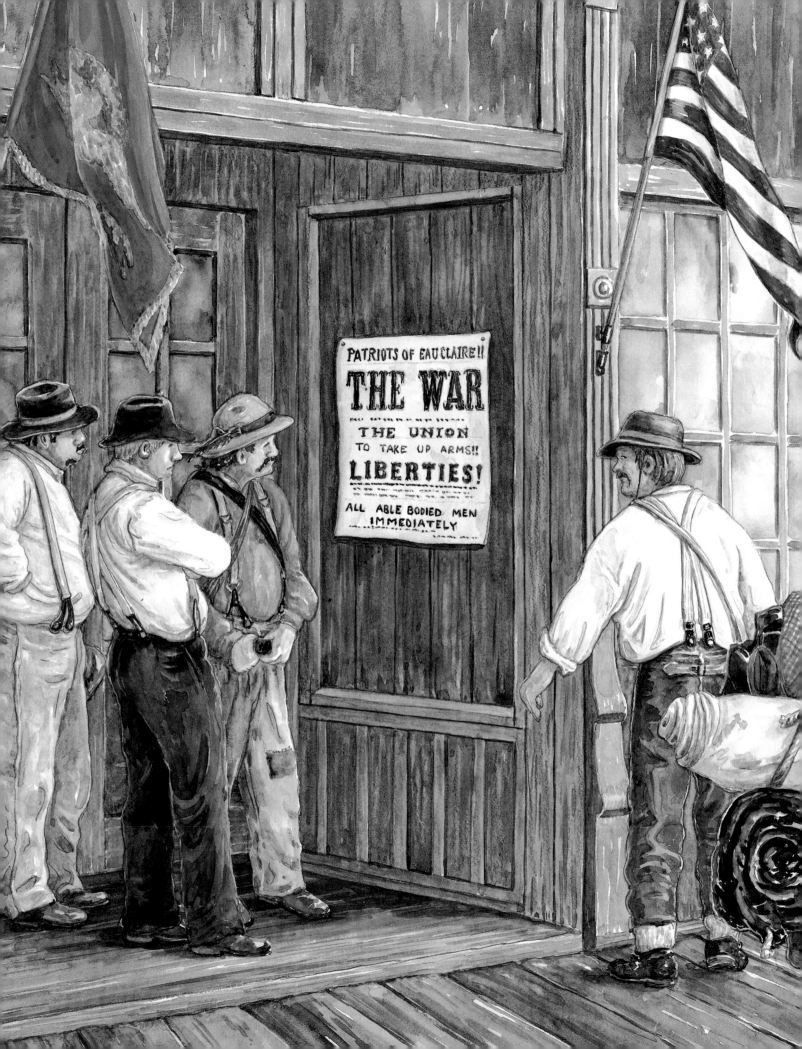

But times were changing. It was 1861 and Abraham Lincoln had recently been elected president of the United States of America. This was a time when northern and southern parts of the country had different ideas about how to be governed. The southern states created a Confederate Army, while northern states created a Union Army. Soon, the two armies were fighting each other in a war between the states.

Folks from Wisconsin began to volunteer for the Union Army and Mr. McCann wanted to do his part. Because he was crippled and didn't believe he would make a good soldier, he decided to send the eagle in his place.

The young bird in tow, Mr. McCann set off to Eau Claire where a group of volunteer soldiers calling themselves the Eau Claire Badgers were organizing for the Union Army. These men came from all over Wisconsin. They were lumberjacks, blacksmiths, carpenters, and farmers.

These men liked the new recruit instantly, and as they were sworn into military service, the eagle was proudly beside them. Afterward, the men changed their name to the Eau Claire Eagles and named their new mascot Old Abe, in honor of President Abraham Lincoln.

The Eau Claire Eagles traveled to Camp Randall in Madison to join other soldiers and form the Eighth Regiment of Wisconsin Volunteer Infantry. People lined the streets to greet them with cheers and banners, and music filled the air. Old Abe was so excited by the celebration that he stretched his wings and grasped a corner of the flag in his beak.

Now at camp the men learned how to be soldiers. As they practiced their drills, Old Abe practiced too. He seemed to like the soldier chosen to be his eagle-bearer and happily sat upon the perch made especially for him. And whenever the bugle called, Old Abe snapped his head to attention, just like his fellow soldiers.

Ready for duty, the Eagle Regiment began to march southward through the countryside. Along the way, people came to see the brigade that carried the eagle, and Old Abe seemed to enjoy the attention very much.

It was not long before the Eagle Regiment met Confederate troops in a fierce battle. With muskets drawn and cannons booming, both sides began to fight. Bullets ripped and sputtered through the air, leaving smoldering trails of smoke and dust.

Now engaged in battle, the Union captain ordered the eagle-bearer to take Old Abe to the rear of the field for safety. But it was too late. **BOOM!** The entire brigade was forced to hit the ground for cover as a burst of heavy artillery fired upon them.

Old Abe screeched loud above the noise and dove off his perch to lay upon the ground with wings spread flat, just like his fellow soldiers.

But there were quiet times, too. Between battles and marches to new locations, the Eagle Regiment would set up camp and remain for long periods of time. Away from families and sleeping in tents with few comforts of home, life in an army camp was not easy.

But even so, they always took good care of Old Abe, giving him good food to eat, a safe place to sleep, and plenty of attention.

During these times, Old Abe kept the soldiers entertained by tipping over water pails, chasing bugs, and sneaking into tents.

One time the eagle flew into laundry as it was hanging out to dry, causing the men to break into laughter. Another time Old Abe stole a fresh chicken from the kitchen tent and led the cook on a chase all throughout the camp.

One private wrote home to say "All the brigade adore Old Abe." Another wrote "Our eagle is the pet of the whole regiment. All think as much of him as we do our colonel and that is saying a great deal."

Old Abe's fame continued to grow throughout the Union troops. When generals or other important officers visited camp, they always tipped their hat to the eagle, causing the entire brigade to cheer. And when this happened, Old Abe greeted them in return by spreading his wings and letting out his best eagle-cry.

But Old Abe's fame was growing throughout the Confederate Army, too. Some Confederate soldiers made fun of the eagle, calling him "Yankee Buzzard" or "Old Crow" whenever they had the chance.

Little did anyone know that when the armies were to meet again, the Confederate soldiers would have a new target. They were going to take the eagle— dead or alive.

The Battle of Corinth began with a siege of fire. The Confederate soldiers fired fast and steady, aiming at Old Abe. The battlefield quickly became a frenzy of sound and smoke as the soldiers fought. Bullets grazed Old Abe, and his piercing cries could barely be heard above the sounds of war.

In an instant, one bullet came his way, snapping the cord that tethered him to the perch carried by the eagle-bearer.

Now free, Old Abe did not fly away. Instead, he flew straight into the heat of battle. With wings spread wide he soared low over his troops and toward the Confederate line, encouraging every Union soldier.

From that day on newspapers wrote stories about Old Abe and his flight into battle. It was not long before Old Abe became a hero among men and women, and a legend throughout the country.

Old Abe served with the Eagle Regiment for three years. Side by side with the troops during 37 skirmishes, the eagle was never wounded. In that time Old Abe had grown from a small brown bird to a handsome eagle with a glorious crown of white.

In September of 1864 it was time to let Old Abe retire from duty, and so he was presented to Governor James T. Lewis. Knowing how important the eagle had become, Lewis said he was proud to accept Old Abe and to care for him always.

When the Civil War came to an end in the spring of 1865, Old Abe attended conventions and fairs to raise money for sick and wounded soldiers. For many years he worked as an honored symbol of our nation's freedom. People would line up for hours to have their picture taken with him.

It was a sad day when Old Abe died in 1881. But even though the eagle was gone, his story remained in the hearts of those who loved him. Because of this, Old Abe, the eagle from Wisconsin, will remain a legend forever.

The grandfather finished his story and the two made their way home. As the boy stepped outside he looked into the sky. From that moment on, his heart told him that somewhere the spirit of an eagle from the woods of Wisconsin was still there, soaring wild and free forever.

"Old Abe belongs to the number of those who have had greatness thrust upon them. The whole country has heard of him."

—*The Milwaukee Sentinel*

To unlikely heroes everywhere. May you always soar free.

KJW

For Ted and Betsy – Just as Old Abe inspired his troops,
from the very beginning you have inspired me.

LC

ACKNOWLEDGMENTS

Laurie Caple would like to thank William Brewster and Abbie Norderhaug of the Wisconsin Veterans Museum; the Wisconsin Historical Society; the Chippewa Valley Historical Museum; and Officer Michael Syphard of the Wisconsin Capitol Police (Wisconsin State Capitol Building).

Sleeping Bear Press

310 North Main Street, Suite 300
Chelsea, MI 48118
www.sleepingbearpress.com

THOMSON
GALE

© 2006 Thomson Gale, a part of the Thomson Corporation.

Thomson, Star Logo and Sleeping Bear Press are trademarks and Gale is a registered trademark used herein under license.

Printed and bound in Canada.

First Edition

10 9 8 7 6 5 4 3 2 1

Library of Congress Cataloging-in-Publication Data

Wargin, Kathy-jo.
The legend of Old Abe / written by Kathy-jo Wargin ;
illustrated by Laurie Caple.
p. cm.
ISBN 1-58536-232-8
1. Old Abe (Eagle)—Juvenile literature. 2. United States. Army. Wisconsin Infantry Regiment, 8th (1861-1865)—Biography—Juvenile literature. 3. Eagles—Wisconsin— Biography—Juvenile literature. 4. Mascots—Wisconsin—Biography—Juvenile literature. 5. Wisconsin—History—Civil War, 1861-1865—Regimental histories— Juvenile literature. 6. United States—History—Civil War, 1861-1865—Regimental histories—Juvenile literature. I. Caple, Laurie A., ill. II. Title.
E537.58th .W37 2006   973.7'4750929—dc22